THUNDER and LIGHTNING

MARY E. EVANS

ILLUSTRATED BY LUIS PERES

To order additional copies of this book, contact:
Xlibris LLC
1-888-795-4274
www.Xlibris.com
Orders@Xlibris.com

To Tim, Jen, Alma, and all the Beatnix
Coffeehouse Open Mic Poetry crew

THUNDER and LIGHTNING
got in a fight.

It happened one dim,
dark Saturday night.

A gang of clouds created
a billowy patch
while the stars lined the clouds
for the ringside match.

5

THUNDER in one corner
was ready to blow

while LIGHTNING
suited up to steal the show.

THUNDER sucked in
his breath deep enough
then belted out a sound
so rough and tough!

LIGHTNING zipped and he zammed,
he zoomed and he zittered,
gliding through the clouds
without a float or a flitter.

LIGHTNING said,
"Shizzle bizzle fizzly hack,"

and THUNDER said,
"Pinga ponga heenga" right back.

LIGHTNING stood tall,
a jagged bronze dagger,

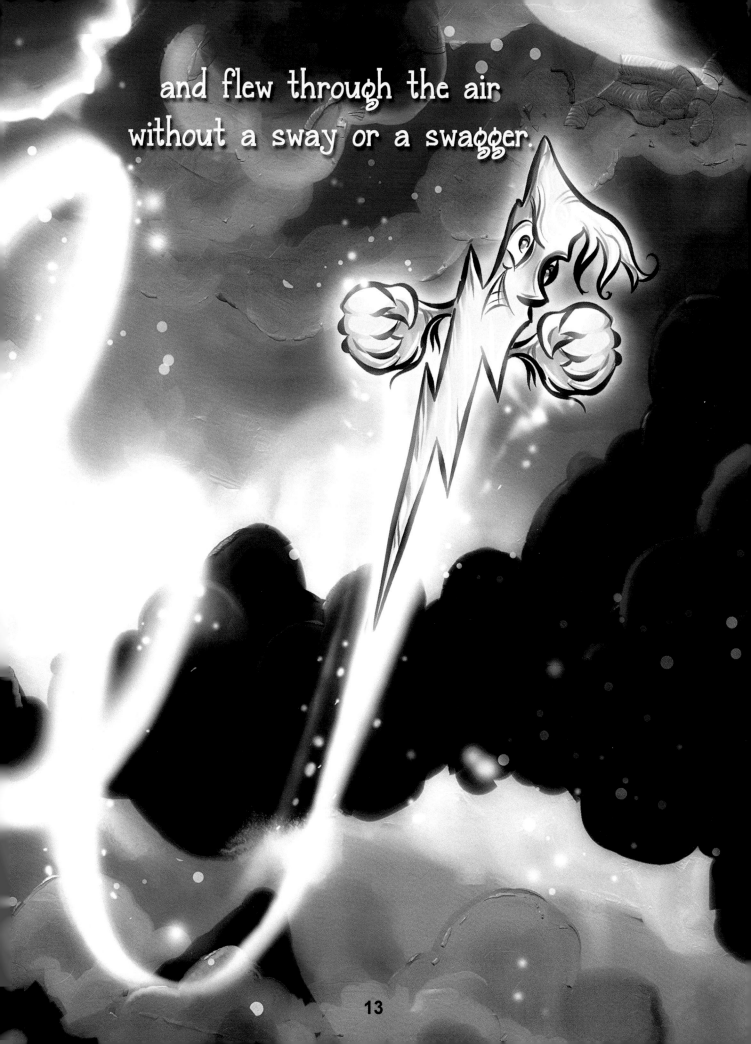

and flew through the air
without a sway or a swagger.

THUNDER had his fists up,
swinging in the air.

LIGHTNING swung his sword
like he just didn't care.

With one huff and one puff,
THUNDER pounded the sky.

With a gold-striped wiggle,
LIGHTNING hissed a war cry!

17

THUNDER swung and he swung,
ba boom ba bomb, ba boom ba bomb!

And LIGHTNING flung
and he flung,
pa cheech che chow,
pa cheech che chow!

While the stars sang a song,
cheering 'em on, singing,
"Who will win the fight?
Who will win the fight?
Who's gonna knock
who out of sight?"

The clouds had their bets
on LIGHTNING to win
while the stars chose THUNDER
as the next kingpin.

21

The battle raged on
'til the break of dawn.

22

The stars nestled in the clouds
began to yawn.

Wait! Who won the fight?
Who won the fight?
Who knocked who
out of sight?

If you really, really, really
wanna know who won . . .

just look up in the sky
and ask the SUN!

Mary E. Evans, aka Maryee, a member of SCBWI, is an avid writer of poetry and lyrical content. She has infused her love for education and enlightenment of others by way of sharing on internet sites and spoken-word appearances throughout the country. A middle school math teacher who loves to find creative ways to reach her students, Mary uses songs and storytelling to engage and ignite learning. Her combined talents have been the driving force behind her first children's picture book, "Thunder and Lightning!"

Luis Peres, professional freelance children's book illustrator, is from Portugal and his work has been exemplified in books, video game design and more. To see more about Peres' handiwork visit www.luisperes.net.

Edwards Brothers Malloy
Thorofare, NJ USA
July 17, 2014